Shamrock's
Seaside Sleepover

Also by Daisy Sunshine

Twilight, Say Cheese!

Sapphire's Special Power

UNICORN
University

#3

Shamrock's
Seaside Sleepover

★ by DAISY SUNSHINE ★
illustrated by MONIQUE DONG

ALADDIN
New York London Toronto Sydney New Delhi

ALADDIN

An imprint of Simon & Schuster Children's Publishing Division

1230 Avenue of the Americas, New York, New York 10020

First Aladdin paperback edition June 2021

Text copyright © 2021 by Simon & Schuster, Inc.

Illustrations copyright © 2021 by Monique Dong

Also available in an Aladdin hardcover edition.

All rights reserved, including the right of reproduction in whole or in part in any form.

ALADDIN and related logo are registered trademarks of Simon & Schuster, Inc.

For information about special discounts for bulk purchases, please contact Simon & Schuster Special Sales at 1-866-506-1949 or business@simonandschuster.com.

The Simon & Schuster Speakers Bureau can bring authors to your live event. For more information or to book an event contact the Simon & Schuster Speakers Bureau at 1-866-248-3049 or visit our website at www.simonspeakers.com.

Book designed by Laura Lyn DiSiena

The illustrations for this book were rendered digitally.

The text of this book was set in Tinos.

Manufactured in the United States of America 0421 OFF

2 4 6 8 10 9 7 5 3 1

Library of Congress Cataloging-in-Publication Data

Names: Sunshine, Daisy, author. | Dong, Monique, illustrator.

Title: Shamrock's seaside sleepover / by Daisy Sunshine ; illustrated by Monique Dong.

Description: First Aladdin paperback edition. | New York : Aladdin, 2021. | Series: Unicorn University | Summary: During Unicorn University's fall break, the four unicorn friends have a sleepover at Sapphire's barn by the sea, but one of Uncle Sea Star's ghost stories seems to be coming true.

Identifiers: LCCN 2020050113 (print) | LCCN 2020050114 (ebook) | ISBN 9781534461710 (paperback) | ISBN 9781534461727 (hardcover) | ISBN 9781534461734 (ebook)

Subjects: CYAC: Unicorns—Fiction. | Sleepovers—Fiction. | Ghosts—Fiction. | Friendship—Fiction.

Classification: LCC PZ7.1.S867 Sh 2021 (print) | LCC PZ7.1.S867 (ebook) | DDC [Fic]—dc23

LC record available at https://lccn.loc.gov/2020050113

LC ebook record available at https://lccn.loc.gov/2020050114

For lovers of sparkles, rainbows, and magic

CONTENTS

1

Up and Away!

Shamrock peered through his thick, black-rimmed glasses at his space-themed backpack. Sprinkled all over the pack were tiny glow-in-the-dark stars, which matched the rest of his room. Bright orange, red, and purple planets hung from the ceiling on strings, and a telescope was arranged by his window, pointing toward the sky. Shamrock was always reading about the discoveries of famous unicorn astronomers, and dreamt of making his own discoveries one day. He *loved* facts and wanted to know how the whole universe worked.

Tapping his front hoof, Shamrock tried to think of what else he'd need for Sapphire's sleepover party. Should he bring the telescope with him? He'd never been to a sleepover before, but he had read about them in books and was pretty sure he knew how it would go. Sapphire lived at the beach, so they would probably explore the seaside caves during the day and study the stars at night. Comet and Twilight, Shamrock's other best friends, would also be there. Knowing Comet, she would bring delicious treats that she had baked herself. Still, Shamrock couldn't help but feel a little nervous. He knew the other three unicorns had been to sleepovers before. He hoped he wouldn't be terribly out of the loop.

Shamrock decided they would take turns with Sapphire's telescope, so there was no need to bring his own. But he did pack his brand-new, very favorite book. Using his horn, he grabbed *1,000 Incredible and Astonishing Facts* from his book hook. When in doubt, he knew he could dazzle his friends with new facts.

"Shamrock! Time to go!" Dad called out.

"We don't want to fly this thing in the dark, remember!" he heard his Pop add.

Shamrock and his dads lived high up on a mountain and used a hot-air balloon for travel. Otherwise it would take weeks to get anywhere!

"Coming!" Shamrock yelled back. At this point, he could only hope he was prepared.

He zipped the pack up with his mouth, slipped his head through the long loop, and hurried toward the front door. Through the door's window, he could see that his parents were already waiting on the lawn. Even though he was used to it, Shamrock was still impressed by the bright rainbow colors of the balloon. It billowed and waved in the wind, looking eager to rise up into the sky. The huge basket was held in place by large ropes attached to spikes in the ground.

Shamrock trotted out to join his family. His dads walked into the basket and started undoing the ropes. Shamrock followed, closed the door behind him, and made himself cozy. Pop, who was always thinking ahead like Shamrock, had loaded the basket with blankets and pillows to make the journey comfortable.

Dad untied the big ropes, and they were off. Floating

high above Sunshine Springs, Shamrock watched the mountains get smaller and smaller as they made their way over little towns and winding roads. To the north, he could spot the hill that Unicorn University, his school, stood atop. But they were headed south to the ocean. They passed fields that looked like his patched-up quilt back home, and they passed by cotton-candy clouds. Shamrock felt his heart soar. He looked up to see Dad adjusting the flame above their heads. Shamrock knew that the flame heated up the air inside the balloon (which he also knew was technically called the envelope) and that hot air was lighter than cold air, which was why hot-air balloons could float! Shamrock smiled at himself. The science of the hot-air balloon was really magical. He loved flying.

Soon enough he could see the sparkling, deep blue ocean waves whooshing and washing over the beach that Sapphire lived by. It was time for Shamrock's first sleepover. A seaside sleepover!

2

Good-Byes and Hellos

The white sand was nearly below them as Shamrock's dad turned down the flame enough to lower the basket over the beach. The sun was low in the sky, painting the clouds different colors, like a big bowl of rainbow sherbet.

"Okay, Shamrock, we're going to dip low on the sand, and you jump out," his dad was telling him. "We'll be back on Sunday to pick you up."

"Have so much fun, Son!" Pop said with a smile. He gave Shamrock a good-bye nuzzle. "We can't wait to hear all about it. And look, there are Comet, Sapphire, and Twilight now!"

Shamrock's heart leapt when he saw his friends running

down the beach to meet him. Finally the basket got low enough for Shamrock to jump out to a chorus of good-byes from his dads and hellos from his friends.

Shamrock tried to tell his friends an awesome sunset fact he'd read about in *1,000 Incredible and Astonishing Facts* when he landed on the beach, but everyone started talking at once. Comet was shouting about a new pumpkin cupcake recipe she'd recently tried, Twilight was trying to tell them about her new art project, and Sapphire was attempting to herd them to the tent. It was a happy, confusing reunion.

Even though fall break had just started a few days before, Shamrock felt like he hadn't seen his best friends in ages. He was so excited to be with them, it felt like he was still floating in the hot-air balloon. His face almost hurt because he was smiling so big.

"You guys won't believe the tent Sapphire put together," Twilight said when everyone quieted down. Twilight had a jet-black coat, and today her hooves were a sunshine yellow. She painted them different colors all the time, and Shamrock always admired them. She lived much closer to

Sapphire than the others did and must have walked over with her parents earlier in the day.

"Let's go now!" Comet, a rose-colored unicorn, cheered. She was floating with anticipation. Really! Comet had the power of flight. When Shamrock asked how she had traveled, Comet told him that she and her uncle had flown over and arrived just before Shamrock.

"Follow me," Sapphire said with a proud grin. The four of them trotted down the beach to a grassy bank where a large, red barn stood.

"That's where we live!" Sapphire said, pointing to the barn with her horn. "But this is where we'll stay!" She trotted over to a big blue tent. Her blue coat matched it so well, she almost blended in.

Wow. Shamrock was impressed by what his friend had done. String lights were hung up around the tent, and brightly colored rugs and pillows were arranged to make a sort of outdoor living room. In front, she'd made a firepit and even put out sticks and buckets of marshmallows. Shamrock only wondered where the telescope was.

"This is so cool," Comet said. "I've never been camping before!"

"I'm glad you like it. I've been working on it all day," Sapphire said. "But the best part is that my uncle Sea Star is in town. He's taking my sisters out on his ship right now, but they should be back any minute. He tells the best stories. You're all going to love him!"

Just as Sapphire finished speaking, a large, gray unicorn came rambling over. He wore his mane in loose braids like

Sapphire's and had one large, gold earring and a red bandanna tied around his neck. He chuckled. "Are you talking about me?"

"Uncle Sea Star! You're back!" Sapphire said.

Shamrock noticed that four miniature versions of Sapphire had followed Uncle Sea Star over to the tent. They were all talking at once about their boat ride, and it was hard to hear what anyone was saying. Shamrock smiled. This was way different from how it was at his home. He and his dads were usually pretty quiet. Sapphire introduced Uncle Sea Star and her siblings—Ruby, Amber, Opal, and Gem—to her friends.

"Okay, everyone! Come inside for dinner," a voice called from the red barn.

Shamrock looked up to see a light blue unicorn with a white mane standing in the open barn door, an apron hanging from her neck.

"Coming, Mom!" Sapphire shouted before turning back to her friends. "Come on! You're going to love my mom's famous seaweed soup." Sapphire was saying that they were going to love a lot of things, and Shamrock believed her. His first sleepover was off to a great start.

The barn's kitchen was huge, with big windows in the ceiling that you could see the first few stars of the night shine through. Everyone was gathered around a long, wooden table that looked like it was made of driftwood. They were so close to the ocean that you could even hear the waves. Well, only when everyone was slurping their soup and not talking. The soup was salty and delicious and unlike anything Shamrock had ever had before.

Comet licked up the last drop from her bowl and leaned back happily. "I have to have this recipe!"

"I know," Shamrock agreed. "Is this a special seaweed?"

"It's from the bay right there. I gathered it this morning," Sapphire's mom told them. "Seaweed is always better when it's fresh."

"You know, I once knew a unicorn who traveled the world and never went anywhere without a jar of salt water from the bay where she grew up," Uncle Sea Star said, pushing his own bowl away from him. "Said it kept her mind fresh."

From there, Uncle Sea Star's story about the unicorn with the saltwater jar took many twists and turns that Shamrock did not find very believable, but he tried to be polite and listen without interrupting. Shamrock couldn't help himself, though, when Uncle Sea Star said the unicorn had lived to be a thousand years old because of the water.

"That's impossible!" Shamrock burst out, surprising everyone at the table.

"Perhaps," Uncle Sea Star said with a grin. "Though, sea legends can have more truth to them than you might think."

Shamrock didn't know what to think, so he looked over at Sapphire, who just shrugged and smiled admiringly at Uncle Sea Star.

After dinner, Sapphire's younger sisters went up to hear a bedtime story from their mom, and Shamrock and his friends went outside to roast marshmallows. Uncle Sea Star built a roaring fire and asked them if they'd like to hear a ghost story.

Comet and Sapphire gave an enthusiastic "YES!" Shamrock thought Uncle Sea Star's stories seemed too fantastical, like they were tales for Sapphire's younger sisters, not older kids who knew things about the world. But when every-one settled on the grass, Shamrock kept quiet and sat down next to Twilight.

The young unicorns waited as Uncle Sea Star gazed into the fire, clearly deep in thought. *Probably making up a story on the spot,* Shamrock said to himself. It was a cloudy night, and the stars peeked through the dark gray wisps in the sky. The waves washed ashore, creating gentle background music, and the peeping bugs got quieter, as if they were getting ready for the story too. The fire glowed brightly in the center of their small circle and crackled here and there. Shamrock had to admit, it *was* the perfect setting for a story. *If only it were true,* he thought.

Uncle Sea Star leaned back against a large boulder. "All

righty. This is the oldest sea legend I know," he began. "I think I first heard it when I was your age."

Here we go, Shamrock thought. *Uncle Sea Star must think we're a bunch of little ponies.*

"Legend has it that for as long as there've been unicorns living by the ocean," Uncle Sea Star said, "the Glowing Horn has been floating along our shores, protecting an unknown treasure. Many, many unicorns have seen it when they've been out at sea. Even I have seen the Glowing Horn on a misty night—"

"Oh, come on!" Shamrock grumbled, unable to keep quiet any longer. "You did not *really* see a ghost."

"Shush, Shamrock," Comet said. "He's telling the story!"

Shamrock felt his cheeks flush. That wasn't very nice of him to interrupt Uncle Sea Star. "Sorry," he said softly.

"It's true, I really did see it," Uncle Sea Star continued. "It was at night, when the moon was but a sliver and the water was as black as ink. At first I didn't believe it either. I thought it was just my eyes getting tired, but I blinked and I rubbed and—sure as seashells—there was a bright Glowing Horn bobbing in the waves. I knew then, as I know now, that the old story says that whoever reaches the Glowing Horn will find unknown treasure."

Uncle Sea Star paused for a moment and looked out to the ocean. The silence stretched on for what felt like forever. Sapphire whinnied impatiently.

"Tell us more about the treasure," Comet blurted out. Even Twilight looked interested.

Shamrock wasn't sure why, but it made him mad that Uncle Sea Star was pretending to tell the truth when this was all make-believe. He couldn't help but push back. "Well, where's the treasure now?" he asked.

Shamrock was pretty sure that was rude too and felt a little bad about it. Uncle Sea Star was being nice, after all. But Shamrock couldn't stand hearing a story so clearly not based in fact. Uncle Sea Star just looked at him and smiled. "I never went after the horn."

"What? Why not?" Comet almost sounded mad.

"Because every unicorn that has been lured into the sea

by the Glowing Horn's treasure has never been seen again!"

All four unicorn friends jumped back. Even Shamrock! Then they giggled at themselves. Uncle Sea Star chuckled along with them. "All right, time for bed, kids. I'll be out in the morning getting some new supplies for my next sea voyage, but I'll see you for dinner tomorrow." With that, he walked back to the big barn. Even if the whole thing was made up, Shamrock had to admit that Uncle Sea Star could tell a good story.

Shamrock was too tired to even suggest looking through a telescope, and he could tell his friends were sleepy too. So he followed Sapphire to the tent, where everyone settled into their blankets and pillows. The others kept whispering about treasure and ghosts. Shamrock was a little annoyed by how they all seemed to believe Uncle Sea Star's story, when he knew they were smarter than that. Soon enough, their conversation ended, and he could hear Comet's soft snores. Shamrock snuggled in with *1,000 Incredible and Astonishing Facts* to read some true stories before falling asleep.

3

Beach Day Blues

The next morning, Shamrock woke up to the sounds of his friends laughing. He sat up, seeing that everyone was still in tangles of blankets and pillows. The morning air was crisp and cool, so Shamrock snuggled back into his own cozy blanket.

"I dreamt about ghosts all night," Twilight was saying, her eyes big. "I kept thinking there was a Glowing Horn in the tent!" She shuddered.

"Out of everyone, I thought you would be the least afraid of ghosts, Twilight," Sapphire said.

"What do you mean?" Shamrock asked, sitting up. He

yawned and put on his glasses. *Maybe Sapphire will be reasonable about this ghost business.*

"Well, Twilight's ability is sort of ghosty. When she's invisible, we can't see her, but we can hear her!" Sapphire explained.

"It is not the same!" Twilight screeched.

Comet laughed. "Of course it's not! 'Cause you're aliiiiivve!" Comet said the last part like she was telling a scary story of her own, and all the friends started laughing.

One of Sapphire's sisters came in to tell them that breakfast was ready. They followed her into the barn for a breakfast of kelp muffins topped with melting butter. Shamrock ate four.

"I'm going to look for the Glowing Horn today," Comet announced as the four friends walked down to the beach.

"Don't do it!" Twilight warned as they wove their way through the tall grass. "I mean, you don't want to be lured out to sea forever, do you?"

"She's right," Sapphire agreed, and looked back at them. She was leading everyone to a special secret beach she'd told them about at breakfast. "All the treasure stories around here

always lead to bad things. Trust me, I've heard a lot of them."

Shamrock took a deep breath. "Guys, there is no evidence that ghosts are real. In fact, these stories usually hide real scientific truths. So they're kind of dangerous. I've been meaning to show you this new book I have, *1,000 Incredible and Astonishing Facts*—"

But Comet didn't let him finish. "Actually, I have a theory about the ghost."

Not only did she interrupt him but she ignored him too. Shamrock felt like she had taken all the wind out of his hot-air balloon, but Comet didn't seem to notice. *Maybe I just didn't say it loudly enough,* he thought.

"The story says you can't go *after* the ghost," she continued, "but what about *inviting* the ghost to shore?"

"Guys!" Shamrock yelled this time. "Ghosts are not real. We know this. However, I've done research on the caves here, and there are stones in there that are way more interesting than any ghost. Some of them even sparkle in the dark, without sunlight! Why don't we go rock hunting instead of ghost hunting?"

Shamrock looked around at his friends, expecting to see their faces lighting up with excitement. But they didn't seem to get it. He felt his heart sink with disappointment.

Sapphire said, "Let's hang on the beach for a little while. I brought a blanket and a hoofball." Sapphire held up her basket so he could see. "There are some cool shells around here, though!"

Shamrock was bummed, but Comet and Twilight were already helping Sapphire set up the beach blanket, and at least this did not involve silly ghost hunting.

"Ooh, and your mom packed us some more of the kelp muffins," Comet said, bringing out her own basket. "I'm pretty sure I'll eat ten today."

They lounged and laughed on the beach, and Shamrock had to admit that it was fun, even if there weren't any special rocks around. He got out his copy of *1,000 Incredible and Astonishing Facts* and showed it to Sapphire.

"This is so cool, Shamrock!" Sapphire was as excited as he was about it. "Actually, I kind of wonder what it says about ghosts."

Shamrock groaned.

"I can tell you about a ghost," Comet told them. "Once, when I was staying at my great-aunt Jupiter's, I was sleeping on the couch, and I swear I saw an old bathrobe dancing on its own in the middle of the night. Just swirling around the living room!"

Twilight laughed so much, she spit out some of her muffin, and Sapphire snorted. But Shamrock was totally over the ghost talk.

"Comet, you know you were only dreaming," he said. "There's never been any evidence of ghosts. It's just stories people like to tell."

"I don't know, Shamrock," Twilight said. "I think I believe in ghosts. I mean, if there are so many stories about them, that's kind of like evidence, right?"

Comet nodded enthusiastically. "Totally, Twilight! Good point."

Sapphire shook her head. "Honestly, I'm with Shamrock. I mean, I've heard sea legends like this all my life, and I love them. But I just think people like to tell stories, and ghosts always make for good ones."

Shamrock nodded, feeling much better. At least someone was on his side. He stood up and kicked the hoofball. "Who wants to play?" he asked.

"Me!" Comet said, and Shamrock passed it to her. Twilight and Sapphire ran down the beach and drew a goal in the sand. Comet and Shamrock did the same where they were.

Comet and Sapphire were on Unicorn University's hoofball team and were better players than Twilight and Shamrock, but it was still fun running on the beach and scoring goals in the sand.

After a while, Comet stopped dribbling the ball to say, "Can we break for some more of those seaweed muffins? All this running has made me hungry."

Shamrock heard his belly rumble. "I wouldn't mind a muffin break," he said.

Twilight took the ball from Comet and tried to kick it in the direction of the picnic blanket, but—oh no!—it went zooming toward Sapphire's head.

"Sapphire, look out!" Twilight squeaked, but Sapphire didn't seem to hear her. She didn't even notice when the ball zoomed right by her ear.

Shamrock saw that Sapphire was staring out at the

ocean. Her face was so pale that it looked like—well, like she'd seen a ghost!

Sapphire shook her head and looked over to her friends. "You guys, you won't believe this, but I think I just saw the Glowing Horn."

4

Follow That Horn!

Sapphire dashed along the beach, toward the direction of the barn. "I think it went this way!" she shouted behind her. "Let's follow it!"

Twilight and Comet galloped after her, with Shamrock following behind. He hoped his book wouldn't get soaked by a wave while he was gone. Sapphire was clearly just imagining things because they had talked about ghosts all morning! No way was there an actual Glowing Horn—today, or ever.

They raced back and forth along the water, everyone peering out to see if they could find the horn again, but no one saw anything.

Finally Sapphire gave up the search and stopped running.

But she still had a huge smile on her face and a glimmer in her eye. Shamrock, like Comet and Twilight, knew that was her adventure face.

"Operation Sleepover Ghost Hunt, am I right?" Comet said with excitement. It wasn't quite a shout, but Comet had a naturally loud voice that always sounded a little like she was yelling at a hoofball game.

Twilight laughed. "This better not be a scary ghost."

"You guys are being way too silly," Shamrock said. This was totally out of control. "Ghosts are not real. I have tons of books that say so."

"You aren't being very open-minded, Shamrock," Sapphire pointed out.

"You were just saying you didn't believe in ghosts!" Shamrock insisted.

"Seems like a lifetime ago," Sapphire said simply. "Not to mention, I just had firsthand experience with one. You know that observation is a basic principle of scientific discovery."

That stopped Shamrock in his tracks. He bit his bottom

lip and nodded his mint-colored head. Perhaps he had been thinking about this ghost business all wrong. Maybe the best way to put this ghost behind them and move on to the caves was to *prove* to his friends that the ghost was all in their imaginations. He gave his friends a serious look that they all knew as "Shamrock Science Mode."

"Okay, let's scientific-method this ghost," he said with a smile.

Everyone laughed and cheered.

"But after we figure out what's going on with the ghost, do you guys promise to explore the caves with me?" he asked.

They all agreed and did a group high-U to seal the deal.

Shamrock said, "Okay, well, we have our scientific question: 'Are ghosts real?'" Everyone else groaned, but he ignored them. "The next step is to gather information."

"Glitter-tastic! We should talk to Uncle Sea Star," Comet said. "Maybe there's some information he left out. Maybe he even knows how to talk to ghosts."

"Let's go meet him in town," Sapphire agreed. "You

guys will love it. It's the oldest town in Sunshine Springs!"

They walked away from the water and through the tall beach grasses. Shamrock was excited. He wondered what kind of old buildings there would be and if there was anything about them in *1,000 Incredible and Astonishing Facts*.

"I'm thinking we should have a nice, polite chat with the horn," Comet said as they walked along the winding lane filled with broken seashells.

"How would a floating horn be able to talk?" Shamrock asked.

Comet shrugged, but Twilight said, "There are more ways to communicate than just speaking. Maybe the horn can spell out words or move objects."

"Very true," said Comet. "So we'll figure out how to talk to the horn, and then we will ask it to join us on the beach. *Then* we will ask it where the treasure is."

"And we won't get lost at sea, because we're luring the ghost to *us*!" Sapphire said. "Brilliant, Comet."

"I don't know," Twilight said softly. "What if we make friends with the ghost and leave the treasure alone?"

"Let's take the scientific method step-by-step. We don't have to worry about the treasure yet," Shamrock pointed out.

The sun was shining, and the ocean breeze was cool. The four friends were enjoying the walk so much that they made it to town before long and were all smiling as they wove their way through the cluster of little wooden buildings.

Shamrock noticed that the whole town seemed to lean east, as if the ocean wind had pushed it that way. Most houses had sea glass windows, with different blues and greens melted together. Unicorns were selling rope, sea-weed, and trinkets from carts that lined the roads. Shamrock saw one unicorn push a cart filled with old books. The pages were browned with age, and it looked like the covers were made of everything from old sails to dried bark.

"Hey, kids! Looking for me?" The friends spun around, and Uncle Sea Star was standing right in front them, a big basket full of rope hanging from his neck.

"Uncle Sea Star, I have incredible news," Sapphire told him in her serious student voice.

Then Comet yelled out, "She saw the Glowing Horn!

She saw the Glowing Horn!" until Sapphire shushed her in an equally loud voice.

Shamrock looked around to see the unicorns of the town peeking at his friends curiously. There was a very old unicorn pushing a cart of glass bottles and iron pots and pans who looked particularly interested. Two unicorns dressed like Uncle Sea Star stopped their conversation and pricked up their ears. Shamrock was curious about what Uncle Sea Star knew too.

"Uncle Sea Star, you have to tell us how to lure the horn to the beach," Sapphire was saying. "Think of the treasure!"

Uncle Sea Star chuckled. "This is a treasure-hunting sleepover, eh? No, no. Too many unicorns have been lost to this legend. You'll just have to let the horn be, niece."

"But I found a loophole!" Comet pressed. "If we lure the horn to us, then the horn can't lure us to the sea." She closed her eyes and nodded seriously, as if settling the point.

Uncle Sea Star just shook his head. Shamrock knew his friends were going about this all wrong. If he were going to be part of this fact-finding mission, then they were going to do things correctly.

"Right now we're just gathering information to form our hypothesis," Shamrock said seriously. "That means 'an educated guess,' by the way. We will not perform any experiments until we get our facts straight, I promise. Of course, we'd rather talk to you about this instead of finding the information someplace else. I mean, some of those

old books over on that cart looked like they might have some information . . . and actually, those unicorns over there seemed interested. . . ." Shamrock drifted off, starting to get lost in thought. He wished they were closer to the library at school.

Uncle Sea Star chuckled and shook his head again. "Okay, okay, but this is just an old story, all right? Might not be anything to it. And all four of you must promise me you won't get yourselves into any danger. Sapphire, don't get me in trouble with your mother!"

Sapphire promised not to do anything dangerous.

Uncle Sea Star nodded and said, "Legend says that the Glowing Horn is always trying to add to its treasure. It's supposed to be drawn to shiny things."

The young unicorns nodded in unison, hanging on his every word.

"The thing is, the Glowing Horn knows unicorns want to take its treasure. Make sure it doesn't see you, or else you could be in trouble with the ghost!"

Twilight sighed.

Sapphire ignored it. "Twilight, I think we'll need to use your special powers."

"I was afraid you were going to say that," Twilight said, shaking her head.

Before any of them could thank Uncle Sea Star for his very valuable information or even say good-bye, he was crossing the street, waving his horn to a unicorn with an eye patch and a very dirty apron.

5

Finding Treasure

O kay, so what do we do to find this treasure?" Comet asked as they walked away from town.

Shamrock said, "Well, we can all agree that we have different theories for how this will turn out—"

"We'll be rich, with treasure!" Comet shouted.

"We'll discover something valuable, at the very least," Sapphire said with confidence.

"We'll make a new ghost friend," Twilight said softly.

Shamrock just nodded. They all knew what his theory was. "The next logical step is to conduct an experiment. Normally this would take weeks of planning, but I'm willing to cut some corners to keep the process moving. Does anyone have any ideas?"

Twilight mumbled, "I think Sapphire does."

"I do!" Sapphire said, nudging Twilight gently with her flank. "We go down to the beach tonight. Twilight will use her invisibility to set out a bunch of sparkly things in front of a fire, so they get, you know, extra sparkly. Then we all hide in the grass and wait for the horn to come to the beach."

Comet whooped and floated, yelling "Best sleepover ever!" again and again.

When Comet calmed down, Twilight finally said, "Okay, I'll do it, but you guys have to promise to stay close by. Also, where are we going to find the sparkly stuff?"

Shamrock's heart leapt right out of his chest. "The CAVES!" he blurted out.

His friends just stared at him.

Shamrock shook his shoulders, straightened his glasses, and tried to get back some scientific seriousness. "Ahem, I mean, there are sparkly rocks in the caves, remember? Perhaps we could gather those."

"Great idea!" Sapphire replied. "I've seen them before, and I think they're sparkly enough to lure the ghost."

"If you guys don't mind, I'm going to skip the caves. I have a surprise for all of us," Comet said with a wiggle of her eyebrows.

"Do you need any help?" Twilight asked.

"Actually, yeah!" Comet said. "That would be great."

The two of them huddled together and made plans during the rest of the way back.

Shamrock and Sapphire walked in silence, as they did quite a lot when they were at Unicorn University. They were both thinkers. Shamrock was usually thinking about a book he had just read, and Sapphire was usually dreaming about where she'd like to travel when she got older.

Shamrock thought that perhaps Comet's surprise would be some sort of baked treat, and he was very much looking forward to it. He was also pleased that he was going to explore the caves sooner than he'd thought he would. Maybe he could go with the flow a little bit more. Maybe.

Shamrock and Sapphire peeled off from Twilight and Comet at the barn and made their way to the beach. On the walk, Shamrock noticed something—or a few somethings—dashing in and out of the grass. He could tell it wasn't the wind, but the little creatures were too quick to see.

"What's that in the grass, Sapphire?" he asked.

"They're ghosts!" Sapphire shouted, making Shamrock almost jump out of his coat. From her *shout*—not because of "ghosts," he assured himself.

Sapphire laughed and nudged him with her flank. Shamrock giggled, but he did wonder if he might have been more affected by all this ghost talk than he'd realized.

"No, not really," Sapphire explained. "They're sand pixies of course."

Shamrock nodded. "Oh, I see! We have grass pixies in the mountains, and they make the same sounds. I've never been able to see one up close, but I've read about them. What about you?"

"Yeah, they're too quick to see. Hmm. You know, I've read about ghosts, too, and now I've seen one!"

Shamrock just shook his head. He could see the caves up ahead and raced toward them. Sapphire followed closely behind.

They both paused at the mouth of the cave and stared in wonder at the sparkling rocks. The sun was shining into the cave, making the floor and walls glimmer and shine like diamonds. Shamrock felt like they had found the treasure without the help of any ghost.

6

To Catch a Ghost

After dinner, Shamrock led the way toward the beach. He couldn't wait to conduct the experiment and prove that his hypothesis was right and the others were wrong. He whistled and swished his tail as he pranced through the grass.

Everyone settled at the spot where Sapphire had first glimpsed the ghost.

"Okay!" Sapphire yelled out in her best organizing voice. "Everyone, get some driftwood for the fire, and pile it here." She pointed with her horn to the small hole she'd dug in the sand.

When they'd gathered enough wood, Sapphire arranged

the pile and made a campfire. Shamrock remembered when she'd learned to do that at school from one of the chefs, Stella. Stella was a dragon and knew tons about fire.

"Shamrock, do you have the sparkling rocks?" Sapphire asked.

He sure did. Shamrock had loved gathering the rocks and was excited to bring them home after all this. Some were huge and white with silver specks, and some were shining gray. A few even had purple streaked through them. He handed the bag to Twilight just before she used her special ability to become invisible. Shamrock, Sapphire, and Comet hid in the tall grasses off to the side. They peered through dark green strands to see Twilight line the rocks up in front of the fire so they would sparkle in the light.

"Beautiful!" Sapphire said with awe.

Everyone nodded as they watched the rocks shimmer. Twilight crept back to the grass and dropped her invisibility.

"Now what?" Comet asked.

"Now we wait," Sapphire told her, and crouched a little lower behind the grass.

Shamrock looked up to see the many constellations in the sky. It was such a clear night, he didn't even need a telescope.

"There's the Big Horn," he pointed out, looking up to the constellation that looked like a triangle made of big, bright stars.

Comet laughed. "At first I thought you meant the ghost was here."

Shamrock laughed too. He could understand the mistake.

"Shh, don't scare the ghost," Sapphire reminded them.

"This is pretty cool, though. I read all about the constellations over break," Shamrock said very quietly. "See the tip of the horn? The very brightest star?"

Comet nodded.

"That points north, and unicorns have used it forever to guide their way. There are lots of stories about it."

"Kind of reminds me of what Uncle Sea Star said earlier," Twilight whispered. Shamrock didn't see the connection between ghosts and stars but decided not to say anything. He didn't want to hurt Twilight's feelings.

"Guys, focus on the water!" Sapphire whisper-yelled. "We don't want to miss the Glowing Horn."

They did focus on the ocean, but still no ghost appeared. Soon their legs were cramped, and they all started fidgeting in the grass.

"Maybe the ghost wasn't real, after all," Sapphire said with disappointment.

"Maybe it's just feeling shy," Twilight told her. They all knew Twilight understood that feeling.

"Maybe you were right, Shamrock," Comet sighed. She walked over to the fire and flopped dramatically onto the sand. "All this for nothing!"

"No way! Not for nothing!" Shamrock shouted. He felt like he had taken a big gulp of warm cider, and he was filled with a warm glow from head to toe. He jumped up with glee and raised his horn high into the air as he trotted around the fire. "The experiment proved that I was right! I told you guys all day. I told you! I'm taking a mental picture of this moment right now."

His glasses had gone askew in his excitement, and he

shook his head back to straighten them. Using his special ability, he filed away a memory movie of the moment.

"Well, I still have my surprise!" Comet said, ignoring his speech. She scooted over a large black skillet of cupcakes she had brought and put it by the fire. "Just to warm them up a little," she explained.

Soon the smell of freshly baked cupcakes filled the air, and it wasn't just Shamrock who was feeling good. *Freshly baked cupcakes, I'm surrounded by my best friends, and I was totally proved right. This might be the best picnic ever,* Shamrock thought.

He smiled and looked out at the dark ocean, and then, all of a sudden, he could see the impossible. His jaw dropped when he saw a Glowing Horn emerge from the ocean and float toward them.

7

Running from Ghosts!

G host!" Shamrock shrieked.

"Come on, Shamrock," Sapphire groaned. "We get it! Stop being mean."

"Yeah, ha ha." Comet rolled her eyes.

"No, no, look, look!" Shamrock said. His eyes felt like they were about to pop through his glasses. "The horn is—"

Twilight looked up to see what Shamrock was pointing at. "Coming right at us!" Twilight squeaked.

"Better get moving!" Sapphire shouted when she saw it too.

No one needed to be told twice. Shamrock scrambled up from the sand to run with his friends back to their tent, leaving the cupcakes and rock treasures for the ghost.

"Didn't we *want* to find the ghost?" Comet, almost out of breath, reminded them as she ran.

"I guess we didn't think about the fact that scary ghosts are, well, scary! So we gotta run faster!" Twilight yelled louder than any of them had heard her yell before.

When they got to the tent, they turned back to see the Glowing Horn still glimmering over the surface of the ocean. Shamrock looked at the tent and felt way too scared to sleep outside.

"Um," Shamrock ventured in a shaky voice, "maybe we sleep in your room tonight?"

"Totally," Sapphire agreed without even pausing to think. They all grabbed their bags and made their way into the big red barn.

Soon they were settled in Sapphire's room—snuggled close together with the lights on—but they couldn't stop thinking about the ghost. Shamrock could feel his friends shivering beside him. Of course, they had wanted to see it, but now they'd didn't remember why! What if the ghost was mad that they tried to trick it? Shamrock took a deep breath to calm down and think rationally. But what was rational about a ghost?

"I don't think I can sleep tonight," Twilight admitted. "We just saw a ghost! And it's still out there!"

"I'm sorry about earlier, guys," Shamrock told them. "I was not being a good friend at all. You were right, and I was so, so, so very wrong."

Comet waved her hoof as if to shoo away the apology. "Honestly, I thought this was just a fun game. I am

as surprised as you are that we saw a ghost!"

"Me too! I am surprised our trap worked," Twilight admitted. "I was only going along with it because I didn't think the ghost was actually going to visit."

"Me too," Sapphire agreed. "I mean, I really did think I saw the ghost at first, but as the day went on, I kinda thought I'd imagined it."

Everyone started laughing at once. Turned out Shamrock wasn't the only one to think the ghost wasn't real, after all! Their laughter broke the tension, and soon enough everyone was able to settle down to sleep.

Shamrock felt a little silly for being so serious about the ghost all day. His friends had just been having fun!

He lay awake longer than the others, not sure what to think about laying eyes on a ghostly being. What did it mean to have Uncle Sea Star's story be real? Had he been telling the truth about other things too? It all made Shamrock's head spin. Eventually, when his head was too full of questions for him to think anymore, Shamrock finally drifted off to sleep.

8

Sweet Discovery

Everything was different in the bright morning sunshine. As he sat up and yawned, Shamrock regretted being scared of the Glowing Horn. And now they had lost their chance to talk to a ghost. *A missed scientific opportunity!*

Shamrock, Comet, Twilight, and Sapphire ate breakfast at their tent that morning. Everyone agreed with Shamrock, that they were silly to have been afraid the night before.

"It's not like it was being mean or anything," Twilight pointed out.

"If anything, it was friendly! Coming over to say hello," Comet added.

Sapphire shook her head. "I can't believe we were all so scared. We totally missed our chance."

"I don't know about that," Shamrock pushed back. He suddenly had a fluttering feeling. An idea was taking shape!

"But our parents are coming to pick us up this afternoon," Twilight said.

"Yeah, we don't have another night to look for the ghost," said Comet.

Shamrock just smiled. "But we don't need to wait for nighttime. Remember, Sapphire first saw the Glowing Horn during the day. Most might think a ghost will only appear at night, but we know that's not true in this case. Even though we're dealing with the supernatural, we can still approach this situation rationally. Now, what else do we know about this ghost?"

Sapphire was nodding enthusiastically. This was the type of adventure she was looking for. "Great thinking, Shamrock. We know the ghost appeared when we put the shining rocks out, like Uncle Sea Star said it would."

"No, wait!" Comet said. "The ghost totally came for my

cupcakes, remember? I mean, they *are* good. You know, I created the recipe myself. My great-aunt had a certain version, but she didn't use cinnamon—"

Shamrock's horn went into the air with a start. "And before that, it came out when we were having a picnic!"

"You're right!" Twilight agreed. "This ghost is hungry."

"And has a sweet tooth," Shamrock added.

"I like this ghost. And I even have more cupcakes!" Comet said. They didn't need treasure or sparkly things to talk with the ghost. They needed sugar!

"Okay, okay," Sapphire said to get the group's attention. "But what will we do this time if the ghost does come back?"

"Not run away," Comet said.

Sapphire laughed. "Yeah, but how do we get it to tell us where the treasure is?"

51

"I think we should record the sights, sounds, and movements of this ghost," Shamrock was quick to say. "This is quite a major discovery, and we must act like scientists. I mean, we could be interviewed for a book—"

"Personally, I prefer to act like a treasure hunter," Comet interrupted.

"Either way, let's just be nice to this ghost, and hopefully we'll learn lots of different things," Twilight said.

"As always, Twilight knows exactly what to say!" Sapphire said. Everyone laughed. They all knew that when Twilight said something, it was worth saying.

The four friends agreed to be nice and welcoming to the Glowing Horn. No one wanted to upset a ghost!

9

The Sweet Tooth

Like his friends, Shamrock carried sweets in a basket down to the beach. Not only did they bring Comet's famous cupcakes but they found cookies and seaweed muffins as well. They wanted to bring a feast to tempt the ghost!

Shamrock's heart fluttered with excitement. He couldn't believe how wrong he'd been earlier. This was quite the scientific discovery. He thought more about what it would be like to be interviewed. Maybe they would meet a famous writer. Or maybe they would write their own book and become famous themselves! He was kicking himself for not using his ability last night. He had only recently discovered that he had a superpowered photographic memory that could take memory movies of what he saw. He could even access other people's memories if he tried hard enough. He would have to remember to ask his friends to describe their own experiences with the ghost to him in detail later.

Down at the beach, the four unicorns laid a blanket down and piled all their treats together. Twilight, always the most artistic in the group, made sure to arrange things so they looked as beautiful as possible.

Everyone waited quietly. At first nothing happened, and Comet started shifting on her hooves, impatient to see the ghost again. Then Shamrock remembered they had been yelling about a muffin break when Sapphire had first seen the ghost.

"Wow, look at all these amazing sweets!" Shamrock shouted at the ocean.

Comet picked up on his thoughts immediately. "Wow,

so many delicious things to eat!" she shouted.

"Never seen so many amazing sweets!" Shamrock yelled.

The four friends wiggled on their hooves and tried not to giggle as they waited. Each looked in a different direction so as not to miss the ghost, and they continued yelling about their sugary picnic.

After what seemed like a long time but was perhaps just a few minutes, the Glowing Horn was back. And floating toward them!

This time the friends stood their ground. They were going to talk to the Glowing Horn.

"Steady, unicorns, steady," Sapphire reminded them. "We are going to stay here and welcome the ghost."

Shamrock felt his heart beating inside his chest as he watched the Glowing Horn get bigger and bigger as it rose out of the ocean. Even though they had decided not to be afraid of the ghost, Shamrock couldn't help but be a little frighted.

The Glowing Horn was becoming much bigger than your average unicorn horn as it moved toward them. And it had that special glow, more like the stars on Shamrock's backpack than the glitter of their own horns. Even in bright sunshine, they could see it glow!

Then, suddenly, Shamrock realized it wasn't a ghost at all.

10

A New Friend

The creature's head broke through the water, revealing the smile of the young blue narwhal floating toward them. "Hey, guys, do you think I could have a cupcake? All I've had is seaweed for *weeks*!"

All four unicorns just stared back in surprise.

"I'm Ned, by the way," the young narwhal said. He raised his eyebrows when the unicorns still didn't say anything back.

Shamrock was the first to find his words. "Hi, I'm Shamrock. Are you a narwhal? We thought you were the Glowing Horn ghost! But it's strange, right? For a narwhal to be in these warm waters? Are you lost? And your

horn is glowing! I've never read anything about narwhals having glowing horns." All his thoughts spilled out so fast, he could hardly breathe. Having grown up in the mountains, Shamrock had never met a narwhal before. Of course, he'd read a ton about them. *1,000 Incredible and Astonishing Facts* even had a whole page about how a narwhal horn could grow up to ten feet long. As always when he met someone new, Shamrock found himself babbling and spurting out facts. It reminded him of when he had met Twilight on their very first day of school.

Ned just laughed at all his questions. "No way! I mean, yeah, I'm a narwhal. But I'm not lost. I'm on vacation with my family. My horn is glowing 'cause of the special water in the hidden caves, you know?"

The four unicorns just blinked at him for a beat.

Then Sapphire finally said, "I've lived by this beach

my whole life, and I've never seen a narwhal around here! And I've never heard of hidden caves." She shook her head. Shamrock thought she would have been less surprised if she really had been talking to a ghost.

Ned laughed again. He smiled as he bobbed a little in the water. "Well, we usually stick to the deeper caves and don't come up here, because the water is so warm and we like the cold. But I kept smelling and hearing about all these sweets, and we've had to eat boring seaweed for weeks now. And, well, I had to see if I could have some treats."

"Totally!" Comet said, sounding like her old self again. "I baked these myself. Cinnamon is the trick to the recipe."

Comet waved at the blanket with her horn, and Shamrock wondered how Ned was supposed to get a cupcake. *He can't walk on sand, right?* Shamrock wondered before shaking his head. *Of course he can't! Be rational. Get a hold of yourself!*

"I think you'll need to toss him one," Shamrock told Comet when he'd cleared his thoughts.

"Would you mind?" Ned asked a little sheepishly. "They do smell good."

Comet tossed him two cupcakes in a row, and Ned caught them both in his mouth and swallowed them whole.

Shamrock started to wonder about the hidden caves. That really would be a scientific discovery for unicorns! He hadn't read about them in any of his books.

"Um, could you tell us about the hidden caves?" Shamrock asked, after Ned had eaten another four cupcakes.

"Actually, I might be able to show you. It's super cool. Everything glows and stuff," Ned told him, his mouth still full. "But I think you'll need a boat. Unicorns can't swim that far, right?"

"No, not as far as narwhals anyway," Sapphire admitted. "Luckily, we do know someone with a boat."

Shamrock looked up to see Uncle Sea Star's boat coming toward them. Somehow Sapphire's uncle always arrived just in time. Shamrock smiled. He was starting to sound like one of the sea legends.

"Ahoy there!" Uncle Sea Star called to them. "A narwhal

in Sunshine Springs? Well, I never heard of such a thing! Captain Sea Star at your service," he said, bowing his head.

"I'm Ned! I was going to show my new friends the glowing caves. Care to give them a lift?"

Of course, Uncle Sea Star was always up for such an adventure. The five unicorns sailed after Ned as he led them farther out into the water. He stopped short in what seemed like the middle of the ocean, and Shamrock wondered what kind of special powers he had to make him see what unicorns could not. But Uncle Sea Star dropped the anchor, and the unicorns jumped into the ocean and swam after Ned. The entrance to the cave wasn't too deep, and they just had to make a quick right before they popped up in a glowing dome filled with natural beauty.

At first Shamrock's glasses were all fogged up from the swim, and he could only see the strange light coming off the walls. When the lenses finally cleared up, he looked around to see his friends talking with other narwhals and exploring the caves. Big rocks gleamed in bright oranges, reds, and purples all over the cave, and strange, friendly fish swam around them. He could see Comet teaching a younger narwhal how to high-U, and Sapphire had her serious face on as she listened to an older narwhal tell her the history of the caves.

Shamrock watched a little glowing, spotted fish use its suction-cup hands to climb out of the water and up the walls of the cave. Miraculously, the same fish flapped its fins to fly through a curtain of glowing vines. Shamrock felt like he was dreaming.

Twilight walked over to him with glitter on her nose. "I've been studying that extra sparkly wall over there," she explained. "I think I'd like to paint a picture of this to remember it all by. Since not all of us have a special photographic memory." She smiled and gave him a little nudge.

Shamrock smiled too. "We really have made an incredible discovery today. It's not even included in *1,000 Incredible and Astonishing Facts*!"

Twilight scrunched her nose and tilted her head. "But we didn't discover this, Shamrock. The ghost story of the Glowing Horn means that unicorns have known about these caves forever. Not to mention how long the narwhals have known about them."

Shamrock was speechless for a moment. Suddenly Uncle Sea Star's words made sense to him. There is truth to the sea legends, even when they seem very untrue! By playing and experimenting with his friends, Shamrock had learned more today than if he had convinced them all to stick to his careful plans. Plus, they had made so many new friends. For a while, Shamrock could only stare at Twilight in wonder, his jaw just hanging open. He shook his head to gain some composure.

"The Glowing Horn brought us to the secret treasure after all!" Shamrock shouted. His old friends and his new friends looked over at him from around the cave and smiled. "Hear, hear!" Uncle Sea Star cheered back.

Shamrock felt like the luckiest unicorn in the universe.

READ ON FOR A PEEK AT

Comet's Big Win

Comet couldn't believe her eyes. Unicorn University had been totally transformed!

Today was the school's Club Fair, and there were tents with waving flags, horns trumpeting joyful music, and cheerful chatter all around her. It looked like a carnival she went to when she was little, but instead of circus performers there were students everywhere. The dance club was performing on stage. The science club was bubbling up purple slime at a booth. There was even a juggling club balancing plates on their horns. All the activity made Comet smile. Growing up in a big family, Comet always felt more at home in big, noisy crowds. She felt like she could wander around all day.

Comet soon spotted her three very best friends huddled together over by the gardening club's table. Plants of every color and shape were piled so high you could hardly see the unicorns in the booth behind them. Shamrock, a mint-colored unicorn with huge, black-rimmed glasses, seemed to be studying a large piece of paper. Twilight, who stood out with her jet-black coat and brightly painted hooves, was looking all around her, clearly distracted by everything that was going on. And Sapphire, a dark blue unicorn with long braids, was pointing to something on Shamrock's paper with her horn. Comet was sure they were deciding which booth to check out next. *I have to tell them about the baking booth!* she remembered. The school's chefs, Stella and Celeste, had told her a secret: the first students to get to the baking club booth would get a special treat! And no one made treats like Stella and Celeste. The fair was already in full swing, and Comet knew they had to get there fast. She started running over but—oh no!—she got a little too excited and her special flying power kicked in. Soon Comet was a rose-colored blur speeding right toward her friends, and with a crash, she knocked them over like bowling pins.

Comet untangled herself from the group while shouting funny apologies. A couple of other unicorns grumbled about the mess, but most unicorns were used to Comet's dramatic entrances. She was still getting used to her magical ability and was always flying into things or accidently floating away.

Comet and her friends got to their hooves, still laughing as the dust settled.

"We were actually just looking for you, Comet," said Twilight.

"Yeah, we were trying to figure out which booth we should check out," Shamrock told her. His glasses had gone crooked in the fall, so he shook his head to straighten them again.

"But don't worry, Comet, I already told them you couldn't join any clubs this year," Sapphire added. She said it matter-of-factly, as if she and Comet had already discussed it.

Comet felt like she had fallen down all over again. *No clubs?!* "What do you mean?" she asked.

"Comet!" Sapphire blew out her lips, giving her friend A Look. "Coach told us last week! Everyone on the hoofball team has be ready for the big game against Glitterhorn College. Which of course means focusing on practice. And nothing else!"

Comet laughed, tossing her bangs out of her eyes. "Oh, come on, Sapphire! We are never going to play in the game. We're just there in case, like, *all* the other players get hurt. We're only first-years!"

Sapphire shook her head and looked determined. "No way! Coach said we could play if we worked really hard."

Comet just shrugged. They didn't have time to get into this when they needed to score one of Stella and Celeste's surprise treats. "We are wasting time, guys! We have to make it to the baking booth!" Comet broke into a brisk trot before there could be anymore hoofball talk. Sapphire had gotten really into it lately and wanted Comet to be as serious as she was. Comet liked running around on the field with her friends, but she didn't really know why the big match against Glitterhorn College was such a big deal.

Sapphire, Shamrock, and Twilight caught up with Comet at the baking booth. She was already munching on an apple oat muffin sprinkled with crunchy sugar crystals.

"Don't tell anyone, but we saved some muffins for you four!" Stella said, handing them each a sugary treat from a basket stashed under the table. Stella was a dragon with beautiful green scales that sparkled in the afternoon sun.

Celeste laughed. "Well, you just said that so loud, you told everyone yourself!" Celeste was a gray speckled unicorn. She and Stella also led the baking club every year, in addition to feeding the whole school.

Stella groaned. "Oh, come on, I'm just excited about these award-winning muffins!"

"So, are you guys signing up for baking club?" Celeste asked them. "It's going to be so much fun!"

"Sorry, Celeste. I've decided on astronomy club," Shamrock told her. "I was thinking about science club, but I think I can only do one thing this year."

"Same." Twilight agreed. "I'm going for art club. Our first project is sculpting! I've never done that before."

"See, Comet?" Sapphire said. "Most unicorns only sign up for one thing. And you already signed up for hoofball."

"Well, I am not your average unicorn!" Comet said. "Where's that baking club sign-up sheet?"

Celeste pushed a clipboard her way, "I hope we can handle you, Comet!"

"You probably can't," Comet said, trying to keep a straight face.

Comet looked up from the clipboard to see Sapphire's most serious face staring right at her.

"Comet, this hoofball game is a big deal. Coach is counting on us!" Sapphire told her.

Comet could see how worried her friend was and was quick to make her feel better. "Really, I can handle both. I'm always sneaking off to the kitchens. This won't be any different!"

Sapphire smiled. "Promise?"

"Super promise with peppermint whipped cream on top," Comet said, giving Sapphire a horn tap.

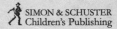

READ & LEARN

with
simon kids

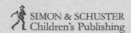

75458